WHO STOLE THE STELLOSPHERE?

Adapted by **Bill Scollon**
Based on the episode written by **Greg Johnson**

ABDOBOOKS.COM

Reinforced library bound edition published in 2019 by Spotlight, a division of ABDO, PO Box 398166, Minneapolis, Minnesota 55439. Spotlight produces high-quality reinforced library bound editions for schools and libraries. Published by agreement with Disney Press, an imprint of Disney Book Group.

Printed in the United States of America, North Mankato, Minnesota.
092018   012019

DISNEY PRESS
New York • Los Angeles

THIS BOOK CONTAINS
RECYCLED MATERIALS

Library of Congress Control Number: 2017961285

Publisher's Cataloging-in-Publication Data

Names: Scollon, Bill, author. | Johnson, Greg, author. | Disney Storybook Art Team, illustrator.
Title: Miles From Tomorrowland: Who stole the stellosphere? / by Bill Scollon and Greg Johnson; illustrated by Disney Storybook Art Team.
Description: Minneapolis, MN : Spotlight, 2019 | Series: World of reading level 1
Summary: When Gadfly Garnett steals the Stellosphere with Miles and Merc aboard, the boys must find a way to thwart the villain and return the Stellosphere to safety.
Identifiers: ISBN 9781532141935 (lib. bdg.)
Subjects: LCSH: Miles from Tomorrowland (Television program)--Juvenile fiction. | Outer space--Exploration--Juvenile fiction. | Space ships--Juvenile fiction. | Theft--Juvenile fiction. | Readers (Primary)--Juvenile fiction.
Classification: DDC [E]--dc23

Spotlight
A Division of ABDO
abdobooks.com

Miles wants to go to the
Adventure Orb.
First he must clean his room.
It looks perfect!

Miles feels bad.
He did not clean his room.
It was a hologram.
He tried to fool his mom.

Mom is not happy.
Miles cannot go to the
Adventure Orb yet.
First he must really clean his room.

SPACETASTIC FACT:
A hologram is like a 3-D photograph.

Gadfly is a robber.

He stole the Rift Drive.

It makes ships go really fast.

Miles's uncle Joe is a Space Guard.
He catches bad guys.
"Give up, Gadfly!" he says.
"Buzz off!" says Gadfly.

Gadfly flies to the Adventure Orb.
Joe follows him.

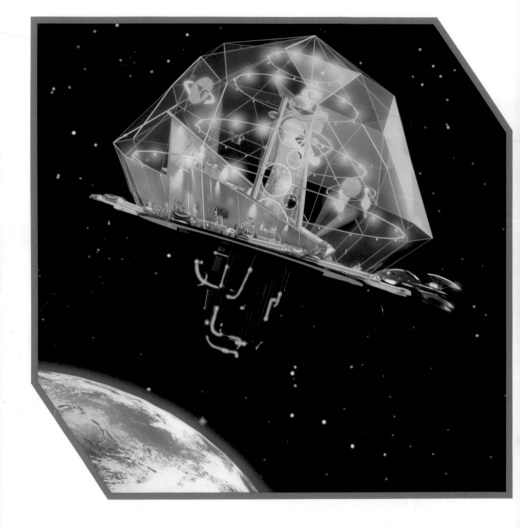

SPACETASTIC FACT:
A space station is in orbit around the Earth.

Miles's family goes to the
Adventure Orb, too.
But Miles stays on the ship.
"Poor Miles," says Loretta.

Gadfly enters the Adventure Orb.
Joe almost sees him.
Gadfly has to hide!

Gadfly looks for a new spaceship.
He peeks into the *Stellosphere*.
"Anyone aboard?" he says.
Miles does not hear him!

Gadfly wants to go home.
His planet is far away.
He wants to use the Rift Drive.

SPACETASTIC FACT:
It would take eight hundred years to fly
an airplane to Pluto.

Miles feels the ship take off.
"Why are we leaving?" he asks.

Joe sees the *Stellosphere* fly away.
Then he sees the Callisto family.

Someone stole the *Stellosphere*!
Mom tries to call Miles.
Screech! The signal is jammed!

"It's Gadfly!" Joe says.
Everyone goes to Joe's spaceship.

They will chase the ship.
They will catch Gadfly.

But if Gadfly uses the Rift Drive, they will not be able to catch him.

"We might never see Miles again!"
says Loretta.
"Don't worry," says Mom.
"I'll find him."

"Go faster, Sheila," says Gadfly.
"I am Stella," the computer says.
"So?" Gadfly says. "We're alone!"
"Incorrect," says Stella.

Gadfly sees Miles on a holo-screen.
"If the Space Guard does not
stop you, I will!" says Miles.

Gadfly makes holo-goons.
"Find that kid!" he says.
Then he takes the Rift Drive to the
engine room.

The Rift Drive is ready.
"Turn it on, Stella," says Gadfly.
But the computer cannot do it.
The switch is in the control room.

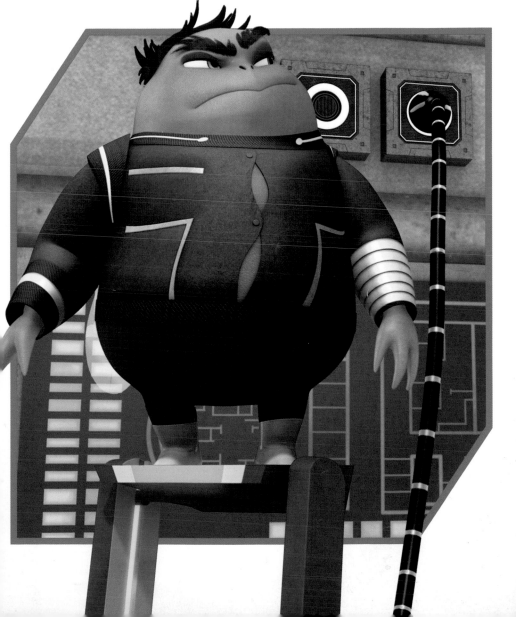

"Power up, Merc," says Miles.
He gives Merc Booster Bites.

A goon runs in!
Merc spits Booster Bites at him.

They go through the goon's
power ring.
The goon disappears! Blastastic!

More goons run in.
"Laserang, launch!" Miles says.
The laserang flies through one
power ring.

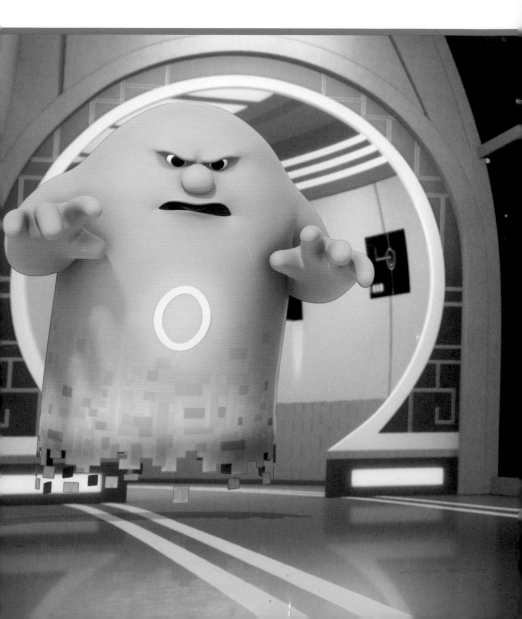

Then it loops back through one more!
One by one, the goons disappear.
"Nothing but hoop!" says Miles.

Miles finds Gadfly.

"Give us our ship back!" says Miles.

"Buzz off!" says Gadfly.

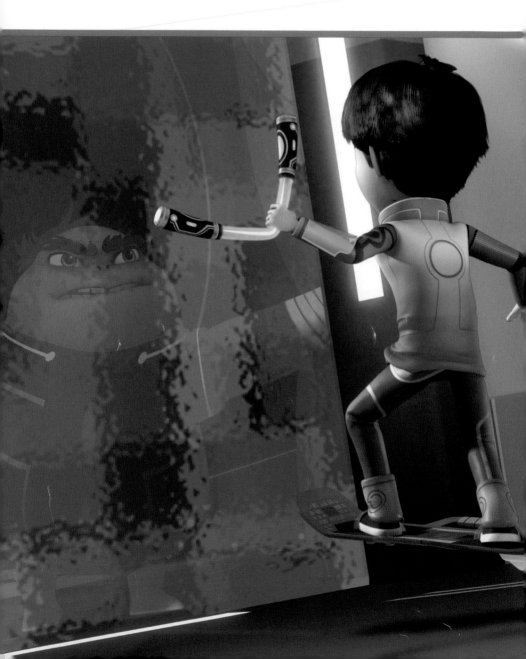

Gadfly reaches for the switch.
But Miles shuts off the gravity!

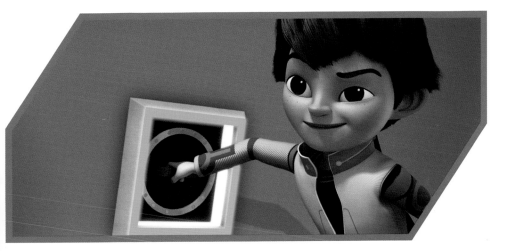

Gadfly floats away.
"No, no, no!" he says.

The Space Guard catches up to
the ship.
*Sun*sational!

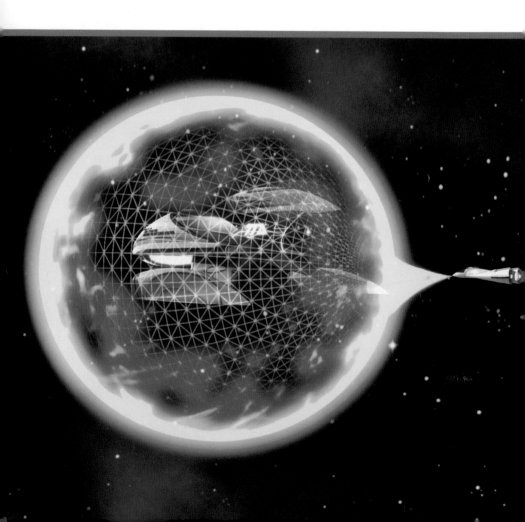

SPACETASTIC FACT:
Our sun is big enough to hold one million
Earths.

Joe has a treat for the Callistos:
a day at the Adventure Orb.
"You too, Miles," says Mom.
"You can finish cleaning later."

BLASTASTIC!